# Who Gives a Hoot?

## Hunter Hoot, the Great Horned Owl.

Linda J. Hawkins

Jennifer Bowles

*Dear Friend of Children,*

**Learning and loving to read is a great accomplishment for early childhood. We can present our children with interesting materials to make this time fun and rewarding.**

The following suggestions can enhance this process:

• Before reading the book, ask the child to read the title and look at the cover to predict what the story is about.

• Read with expression, enjoying this time with your child.

• Pretend to become the character and express and read the same way the character would express him/herself.

• Read a page and allow the child to repeat, mimicking your expression and inflection.

• During the reading, encourage younger children to pick out letters and older children to sound out new words they do not recognize right away.

• Help the child to use phonetic skills to sound out new words.

• Do not pressure the child if they struggle with a new word. Offer assistance. They may remember it the next time they see it. You want reading time to be a positive experience.

• Encourage the child to read to others, brothers, sisters, or to pretend their baby dolls or bears are their audience. They feel grown up while doing this. They can learn while assuming the role of the teacher.

• Ask questions about the book, encourage discussion, and laugh together as you share the funny parts of the story. Ask "Did you learn anything new from the book? Who or what was your favorite part? What good or bad decisions were made?"

Heart to Heart  Publishing, Inc.

Heart to Heart Publishing, Inc,
528 Mud Creek Road • Morgantown, KY 42261
(270) 526-5589
www.hearttoheartpublishinginc.com

Printed in USA

Copy Editor: E. Douced
Editor: Pearl Dexter
Designer: April Yingling

These books are available at a special discount for bulk
purchases for fund-raising efforts, sales promotions, or
educational use. The author is available for speaking and
book signings. Call toll-free 1-888-526-5589
or visit www.lindajhawkins.com.

To all children who
appreciate God's creation
and respect his creatures.

~ LJH

.................

To my children, may you
always be willing to try
something new.

~ JB

Hunter Hoot, a young owl, flew out of the woods. He thought, "I'll hunt and explore a little by myself. With the name Hunter Hoot, I'll need to work hard to be the best hunter in the forest."

He'd been receiving hunting lessons from his mother. They'd been out ALL night searching the forest and nearby fields. He was learning the ways of the woodland night animals.

The great horned owl is the second largest North American owl.

5

The sun was now coming up. As he sailed through the air, he spotted something moving near the Barkleys' farmhouse. He swooped down for a closer look. Now, being new to this soaring business, he failed to reduce his landing speed correctly.

He bumped into the henhouse, knocking himself out. There he lay limp on the ground. He DID NOT know that things were about to change for him.

Baby owls are covered with hair or soft feathers called DOWN.

7

Kelsey Barkley had come to spend the week on the farm with Nana and Papaw Barkley. She was heading to the henhouse to gather eggs when she saw little Hoot fall. Being an animal lover, she rushed to pick him up.

"Poor little thing. I'll take you to Nana Barkley. She's a good nurse. She will know what to do," cooed Kelsey as she headed back toward the house.

Kelsey and the little owl had reached the back side of the farmhouse when the kitchen door swung open. They were suddenly hit with an unexpected blast of water.

Nana Barkley had opened the kitchen door to throw out the leftover water from last night's water bucket. Papaw always brought fresh water in once he'd finished milking the cows.

To Kelsey's surprise, she and little Hoot received a soaking. She felt him move in her hands. Brushing the water from her eyes, she looked down just as little Hoot shook his head. He opened his large, round eyes and peered into Kelsey's surprised face.

Owls have big, saucer shaped eyes, set in a flat, round face. Big eyes help take in more light for night vision.

"Oh, dear! Oh, dear me, Kelsey," cried Nana Barkley. "I thought you were at the henhouse gathering eggs."

"Look what I found! Isn't he the cutest thing with these big eyes and soft feathers? He flew into the building. I think he's hurt himself. *Do* you think we can help him? *Will* he be okay? *Can* I keep him, Nana? *Please?*"

Nana Barkley chuckled. "PLEASE slow down, child! One question at a time. You two look rather wet, but the water seems to have brought your little friend around. Come on and we'll get you dried off."

The great horned owl grows to be a large, powerful bird.

After drying off and changing her clothes, Kelsey decided to dress Hunter Hoot. She put her pretty pink doll dress on him. By now, Hoot wanted to get back to his forest friends and home, but when he tried to raise his wings, he couldn't move.

He sat thinking, looking around the kitchen. If only I'd stayed in the forest and gone to sleep, I'd not be in this tight thing! I wonder what I've gotten myself into?"

The great horned owl can grow to be over two feet long and have a wing span of 36-60 inches.

Kelsey looked at his large, weary eyes. She said, "You must be hungry. I'll feed you some eggs and biscuits."

Hunter Hoot was thinking, "I'd rather have a fresh rabbit or a tasty mouse. They are my favorite foods. Even a skunk would be better than what she's poking into my mouth." He felt miserable.

When everyone had finished eating, Nana cleaned the kitchen. Papaw went to cut hay, and Kelsey decided to put her doll's socks and shoes on Hoot to take him outside.

He was feeling so-o-o sleepy and sick.

The Horned Owl will eat many small animals, including skunks, porcupines, raccoons, rabbits and Canadian geese, but they prefer rodents such as mice.

17

"You've got the longest toenails!" exclaimed Kelsey as she tried to put socks on him.

Nana Barkley laughed. "Those are not toenails. They are called talons. All owls have long, sharp talons. They use them for catching their prey."

"Pray? Owls *pray?*" exclaimed Kelsey.

"No, no!" laughed Nana. "They catch their *prey*. That means they catch live animals for their meals."

They have sharp hooked claws called talons (Tal-uns).
They hook prey tightly in these special claws.

*"Ugh*, hairy live meat to eat!" cried Kelsey. "How can they eat that?" As she looked over at Hoot, he barfed scrambled eggs and biscuits onto the pretty pink dress and Nana's clean kitchen floor.

Nana said, "Kelsey, maybe you should set him free." But Kelsey wanted a playmate, and he was the right size for her doll clothes and her stroller.

Owls have hooked beaks, which help with eating their prey.

Kelsey removed the dirty clothes, socks, and shoes. Hoot was so-o-o sleepy. He couldn't stay awake.

The next thing he knew, they were headed outside in a doll stroller. She pushed him down a bumpy driveway.

He was trying to sit up, but couldn't keep his balance. He was bouncing all over the doll stroller.

The great horned owl hunts at night and sleeps most of the day

They stopped under a big oak tree next to Kelsey's playhouse. Hunter Hoot was so sleepy. He napped once more while she was putting her doll into the swing.

Hoot dreamed he was being stuffed into another doll dress. He recalled one of his mother's instructions. "If you become frightened or angry, make yourself look fierce and large by fluffing your feathers." So he did just that.

"Ah," he thought. "I look fearsome!"

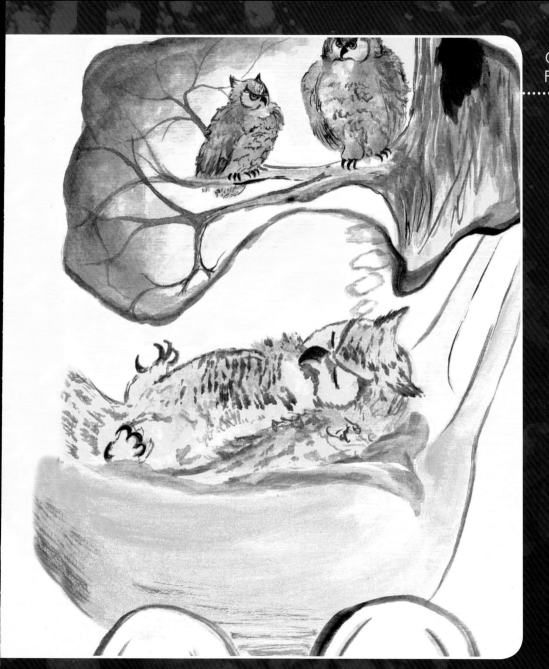

Owl feathers are thick and warm. Owls can and do sometimes fluff up their feathers to look bigger, especially when threatened.

He awoke as Kelsey jerked him out of the stroller. She asked, "*What on earth has happened to you?* I need to brush your feathers down. We're going to have a tea party."

Hoot closed his eyes again and thought, "This has to be another bad dream. ME at a tea party! I'm so-o-o sleepy, I'm . . ."

The eyes of owls take up most of the space in their skull, leaving space for only a thimble-sized brain.

Later, after the evening meal, everyone sat on the porch. Kelsey had set Hoot upon the porch swing beside her. He looked so-o-o sad. His big eyes searched the trees for his mother.

Papaw Barkley asked, "Kelsey, do you see how sad your friend looks? Don't you think it would be best to set him free? He was born and raised in the forest and living with people is something he knows *nothing* about."

The great horned owl raises its babies in late winter. Its feathers keep the eggs and baby owls warm. It is one of the earliest nesting birds in North America.

In the distance, an owl hooted loudly. Little Hunter sat up quickly. He answered, *"Whoo-hoohoo-hoo-hoo."*

Kelsey cried, "That's the first sound he's made all day!"

Perhaps that's his mother calling from the forest," said Nana. "She's ready for her nightly hunting trip, but doesn't see her little hunting partner."

They are often called HOOT OWLS because of the sound they make: Whoo-hoohoo-hoo-hoo!

Kelsey thought, "My mom and dad will be back to pick me up. I'd be sad if I couldn't live with them."

She looked at little Hoot, picked him up, carried him into the yard and kissed him on top of the head. Then she set him down on a tree stump. He looked around as Mother Owl called once more, *"Whoo-hoohoo-hoo-hoo."*

Owls' ears are very special. They can hear the softest sound, such as the squeak of a mouse one-half mile away.

Hunter Hoot stretched his wings and lifted himself high into the air. Kelsey smiled, blowing him a farewell kiss. *"Little Hoot, I'm so glad you spent the day with me!"*

Little Hoot looked down, but he didn't look back. He was not planning on making that mistake again!

Owls have special feathers that do not make wind sounds. Prey cannot hear the owl as he flies down to capture them. Owls can fly 40 miles per hour.

# ANIMAL SALADS

Two of the great American horned owl's favorite foods are tasty mice or rabbits. Creative salads are easy to prepare. With the help of an adult, make yourself a tasty mouse or rabbit salad. They may become one of your favorites, too.

### Mouse Salad

Place shredded lettuce onto a plate. Add two tablespoons cottage cheese in center, and place a canned pear, rounded side up, over cottage cheese. For ears, use almonds, and for the eyes, use small pieces of olives. The nose can be tiny pink candy. Use a long thin slice of licorice or a curled pipe cleaner for the tails and toothpicks for whiskers. Serve with cheese cubes placed on the lettuce. You may add crackers or vanilla wafers.

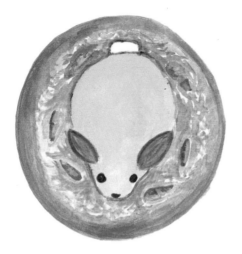

### Rabbit Salad

Place shredded lettuce onto a plate. Add two tablespoons tuna or chicken salad in center, and place a canned pear, rounded side up, over the tuna or chicken salad. For ears, use almonds, and for eyes, use small pieces of olives. The nose can be a tiny pink candy. Use a small bit of marshmallow for the tail. Place baby carrots on lettuce. Serve with crackers.

**These salads are good and nutritious, to keep you hopping!**

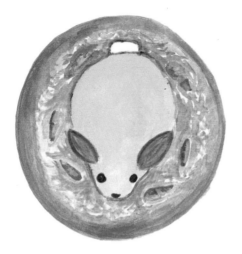

OWL
FACT

Owls have very little peripheral (side) vision. Owls can spot a mouse two hundred yards away. That is the length of a football field.

# Little Hunter Hoot

Little Hoot wanted to explore on his own;
Not going to far from home.
He soon discovered that plans can change.
No longer free, he surely felt strange.
He'd made a mistake with his landing gear.
Now all he felt was sudden fear.
He was quickly stuffed into a pink doll dress,
This left him feeling awesome distress.
Food was shoved into his mouth,
things he never ate.
"A skunk would be better than this kind of bait.
I'm sleepy, so sleepy, just let me go."
But Kelsey says, "Oh, please, Grandma, no!"
After a very long day of living with folks.
Little Hoot was glad grandpa spoke, "Let'm  go?"
She kissed him gently on top of the head.
He flew straight to get into bed.
"A great hunter, I am. I'm Hunter Hoot.
But never again will I take that route!"

*Hunter Hoot on his way out for a school visit/and stopping by the library to visit with a children's' reading group.*

## Helping a Child by Sharing and Learning Together

For a weekend or rainy day project, help your child make a birdhouse, nesting box, or feeder for your feathered friends. Patterns are easily obtained from the library. This gives you quality time, fun learning, and a self-esteem building course for your child.

After reading **Who Gives a Hoot**, plan a drive to a wildlife reserve or a zoo. Take along a picnic to enjoy. As you stroll through the areas, share information and conversation about the animals and birds, such as the great American horned owl. We retain greater knowledge when adding this dimension of learning with our reading sources.

## A Message from Your Forest Friends

Each spring and summer, many baby animals are picked up by people trying to help what they think is an orphaned or abandoned animal. Quite often, the animal doesn't really need any help, because it may be learning to fly or hunt for the first time on its own.

If you find an animal that looks as if it has been left alone, the best thing to do is to leave it alone. Its parent may be waiting for you to leave before it comes back.

Injured animals can be very dangerous because they don't know you are trying to help. Specially trained people like veterinarians and wildlife rehabilitators may be able to help, but it is a good idea to call them and ask what to do before you pick something up. State wildlife agencies usually keep a list of these people in your area who can help.

Never try to keep a wild animal as a pet. It will always be wild no matter what you do. In most states it is illegal to keep a wild animal at home. Help keep wildlife wild by enjoying them from a safe distance.

Darrin Samborsk
U.S.D.A. Forest Service
Land Between the Lakes
100 Van Morgan Drive
Golden Pond, KY 42211

**Because owls have 14 vertebrates in their neck they can also turn their heads completely upside down.**

# Bestseller & Award-Winning Author

**Linda J. Hawkins** is the author of *Alexander and the Great Berry Patch, Alexander and the Great Food Fight, Alexander and the Great Vegetable Feud, Alexander Enjoys His Fruits & Vegetables,* and *Alexander's Enrichment Activities.* Hawkins' work has traveled nationally and internationally. She is also the author of *Catering to Children with Recipes for Memorable Teas* and winner of the USA Book News Award and the Benjamin Franklin Silver Award winning specialty book for *The Unspoken Language of Fans and Flowers with Recipes.*

Hawkins lives in Kentucky. She loves cooking, photography, especially nature and wildlife, and sharing with others. For more information, pay a visit to her website www.lindajhawkins.com.

# Illustrator

**Jennifer Bowles** is a resident and local artist in Western Kentucky. She blended her knowledge and artistic talent with her love of children to create a wonderful art program at Drakesboro Elementary School that began in 1994 with Jennifer as the instructor. She is illustrator of both *Alexander and the Great Food Fight and Alexander and the Vegetable Feud.* Both books were published by Heart to Heart Publishing, Inc.